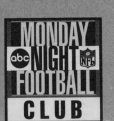

QUARTERBAC
EXCHANGE

I Was John Elway

GORDON KORMAN

HYPERION PAPERBACKS FOR CHILDREN

NEW YORK

Printed in the United States of America.

First Edition
1 3 5 7 9 10 8 6 4 2

This book is set in 12-point Caslon.

ISBN: 0-7868-1236-2
Library of Congress Catalog Card Number: 97-71801

Contents

The Monday Night Football Club

The new trick play was called the Wigwam Aerial Skate-Bomb.

"Hut—hut—*hike!*" bellowed Nick Lighter, the quarterback.

He tucked the football under his arm and scrambled up to the top of the jungle gym in Wigwam Park. He steadied himself, reared back, and threw.

The ball sailed through the middle of the tire swing, up, up, and over the big tepee fountain toward . . .

Down the paved path rolled his receiver, Coleman Galloway, kicking like mad to speed up his skateboard. He looked up, and saw the ball streaking toward him. What a perfect throw! Nick had the strongest arm in the Monday Night Football Club.

Coleman held out his palms to make the catch.

Elliot Rifkin came out of nowhere, sprinting at top speed. Elliot was the defensive back on the Wigwam

Aerial Skate-Bomb. It was his job to break up the play.

Wham!

Coleman and Elliot collided head-on. Coleman went flying off his skateboard. Elliot landed with a crash on top of him. From the grass, four hands reached up frantically for the pass. It was a tie. The ball was caught crisply by both friends at the same time.

"Interception!" cheered Elliot.

"Interception?" Coleman glared at him. "I've got it! It's a touchdown."

"*I've* got it," Elliot insisted.

There was a tug-of-war as the two got to their feet. Each was still firmly clamped on to the ball.

Nick jogged up with Coleman's skateboard under his arm. "What happened? Did we complete the Wigwam Aerial Skate-Bomb?"

"Yes and no." Elliot grinned.

Nick stared at the double catch. "I wonder what the call would be if it happened in a real NFL game."

"Pass interference," Coleman said positively. "And maybe unsportsmanlike conduct, too."

Nick punched the ball loose and picked it up himself. The three friends shouldered their knapsacks and sleeping bags and began walking toward Nick's house. Elliot conducted the traditional postgame "interview."

He thrust out an imaginary microphone. "So tell me, Nick, how does it feel to be the first quarterback in history to throw a touchdown and an interception on the same pass?"

"What can I say?" Nick replied. "I'm awesome. I want to thank my mom and dad, but not my annoying sister. Most of all, I want to thank the great John Elway for being my idol."

"There was a flag on the play," muttered Coleman as they rounded the corner up Nick's front walk. His jaw throbbed, and so did his mood.

"And now, a word from our sponsor," Nick joked on. "Hi, all you sports fans out there in TV land. If you want to throw touchdowns like me, you should eat Cocoa Cruncherooskies Cereal. Sure, it tastes like sawdust, but I'm a big star, and they're paying me fifty zillion dollars to say that it's good."

Out of three serious football nuts, Nick was the ultimate superfan. Maybe it was because of his initials— N. F. L. for Nicholas Farrel Lighter.

It had been Nick's idea to form the Monday Night Football Club in the first place. The organization had one purpose: to make sure none of its three members missed *Monday Night Football* on TV.

Nick, Elliot, and Coleman knew that *Monday Night*

Football was the biggest and most exciting game of the week. But their parents complained that the broadcasts sometimes went on until midnight, or even later. A compromise had to be reached, and the Monday Night Football Club was born.

The three members met each week at one of their houses to watch the game from their sleeping bags in front of the TV. That way, they could be in bed right at the closing gun and get a good night's rest for school on Tuesday.

"Or," as Nick put it, "at least a solid four hours."

It was true. After a good game, the three members could be up half the night reliving every touchdown, field goal, and sack.

Tonight, Nick's living room was the spot. He was doubly excited as he ushered his two best friends inside. This week's matchup featured the Denver Broncos on the road against the New York Giants. John Elway, his favorite player, was a Bronco.

"This is going to be awesome!" raved Nick. He tucked away the football and began to slalom down the front hall, decking out imaginary tacklers. "I can't wait to see Captain Comeback—he's flushed out of the pocket! He scrambles! Wiggles! Dipsy-doodles—"

A large figure clad in dark denim stepped out of the kitchen to block his path.

Wham!

Hilary, Hilary, Heavy Artillery

It was like running into a brick wall. Nick bounced off his eighth-grade sister. As he crashed to the floor, he fumbled the ball, which spun and rolled back down the hall to Coleman and Elliot.

Both boys snickered. "Hilary, Hilary, Heavy Artillery," they chorused in whispers.

Hilary Lighter had grown six inches in the months since her thirteenth birthday. She towered over her brother and his friends.

"I heard that." She grinned at Coleman and Elliot. "Come on in, guys. I forgot that the Get-a-Life Club was meeting here this week."

"That's *Monday Night Football* Club!" roared Nick, scrambling back up.

"Whatever." She led them into the kitchen, where she poured two tall glasses of soda for Coleman and Elliot.

"What about me?" Nick demanded.

She glared at him. "You've got arms. Hey, a package came for you today."

"Wow! Really?" Nick was excited. The only mail he ever got was marked OCCUPANT. "What is it?"

"How should I know?" snapped Hilary. She turned back to Coleman and Elliot. "So, which one of you ladies' men is taking me to the big dance next week?"

"But I thought you were going with Seth Kroppman," blurted Coleman.

"Shhh!" hissed Elliot.

"What? How could you know that?" She looked daggers at Nick. "Have you been spying on me again?"

But Nick was already ripping into the shoe box–size package. "Maybe if your phone voice wasn't as loud as an air-raid siren, the whole neighborhood wouldn't know your business."

He pulled out a letter that was printed on official-looking stationery. "'McArthur, McWirter, McGinty, and McCoy?' Who's that?"

"Sounds like a law firm," suggested Elliot. "What do they want with you?"

Nick read aloud:

Dear Mr. Lighter:
   As you may recall, I am the lawyer who

handled the estate of your late grandfather, Raymond Lighter, two years ago.

We recently moved our offices to a new location, and a secretary discovered an item belonging to your grandfather. It was in a locked strongbox in the rear of a wall safe behind several stacks of documents. I cannot explain how it got there. But a check of the last will and testament revealed that Mr. Lighter wanted it to go to his only grandson.

My apologies that this article is so late in coming.

Yours very truly,
Horace McWirter

Nick reached into the package and pulled out an old brown football jersey.

"Wow!" breathed Hilary. "That must be Grandpa's college uniform."

Nick held it up. Light shone through the holes where moths had eaten through the fabric over the years. The number, in faded orange, was 13.

"Hey, Nick," said Coleman, "how come you never told us your grandfather was a football player?"

"Because he wasn't," Nick replied. "Not in the NFL

anyway. He was a lineman for the North Brainerd Eskimos—some tiny frozen junior college way up in Minnesota."

"Frozen is right," put in Hilary, running her hand along the sleeve. "Check out this material. It feels like mastodon fur."

"It's still cool," Elliot argued. "I mean, real college football. He had to be pretty good."

"He knew *nothing* about football," Nick complained. "He called the modern players pampered babies who made too much money. He hated the touchdown dances, the superstar hype, the TV interviews, the commercials for cereal and shoes and stuff. He thought football was about sacrifice and determination and hard work."

"But a lot of older folks say things like that," put in Coleman.

"You guys just don't get it. Our grandfather was amazing! He was one of those people who could fix a car engine with a wad of chewing gum, and grow carrots out of a brick wall. He knew about tons of stuff. I really looked up to him, but—well, we never agreed on football. We used to fight all season. I—" Nick shook his head. "I guess he didn't like me very much."

"Don't be a doofus!" snapped Hilary. "If Grandpa

didn't like you, how come he told the McLawyers to send you his shirt?"

Nick's face grew wistful. "It's not much of a present. A beat-up old rag."

"Then can I have it?" asked Hilary, taking the sweater from his hands.

"No! It's mine!" He snatched it back and pulled it down over his head.

It was the itchiest article of clothing Nick had ever put on his body. Instantly, he began to sweat. He felt like his skin was crawling with ants. His brain cried out, *Take it off! Take it off!* But he could almost hear his sister's claim on the sweater: "Well, since *you* won't be wearing it . . ."

He clenched his teeth and fought off the urge to scratch.

"Come on, guys." It wasn't easy sounding natural. "Let's set up our sleeping bags for the game."

He led them away from the kitchen. As soon as Hilary was out of sight, Nick whipped the sweater over his head. "Oh, man! Get it off of me!"

Elliot laughed. "You wimp. It can't be *that* bad." He took the brown jersey from Nick and shrugged into it himself.

It came off half a second later. "I used to think the

most uncomfortable shirt on earth was the toxic turtle-neck I got from my Aunt Jenny when I was six," he said painfully. "Well, this blows it away!" He held out the uniform to the third member of the Monday Night Football Club.

Coleman wouldn't even touch it. "Oh, no. Not me."

"Afraid of a little itch?" Nick grinned.

Coleman glared at him. "It's number 13! Bad luck! We've got the big field trip to Overlook Outdoor Center this week. You want me to hex myself and wind up lost in the woods?"

"But it's okay for us?" Elliot demanded.

"You guys aren't as jinxed as me to start with," Coleman said feelingly. "I'm always hanging by a thread. It wouldn't take much for me to get eaten by a bear."

"It would take a bear," Elliot pointed out. "And there aren't any at the outdoor center."

"How do you know?" challenged Coleman. "My luck, a whole new family of bears just moved into the neighborhood."

Nick sighed. "There's nothing wrong with your luck. At least *you* didn't just inherit the world's grossest sweater—from a grandfather who couldn't have cared less about John Elway!"

Are You Ready for Some Football?

"You know the rules, boys," announced Nick's mother. "Pizza boxes in the garbage by kickoff time."

"Yes, Mrs. Lighter."

Coleman and Elliot rushed to clean up the family room before the start of *Monday Night Football*. The North Brainerd Eskimos jersey had served as a picnic blanket for dinner. It already bore several pizza stains.

"Anything has to be an improvement," was Elliot's opinion.

Nick was on the phone with his father, who worked the late shift as a security guard. Usually they discussed the big game. But tonight there was another subject on Nick's mind.

"Remember the time before Grandpa died when we were all watching the game, and John Elway threw that sixty-yard touchdown with eight seconds to play?"

"Mom told me about the shirt," Mr. Lighter said from the other end of the line. "I guess you've got Grandpa on the brain."

"Remember how Elway was jumping up and down?" Nick went on. "And when I jumped along with him, Grandpa got mad at me?"

"You have to understand how Grandpa felt," his father told him. "He played for no money and no glory. The field was usually frozen solid, and every tackle must have felt like a train wreck. Even the marching band was in pain from having their lips freeze onto the mouthpieces of their instruments."

"Grandpa threw my Broncos hat out the window that day," Nick reminded him.

Through the receiver, he heard his father sigh. "And he apologized, Nicky. He had a hard time getting used to the hype and the million-dollar salaries. Please don't be too hard on him. He was a crusty old character, but he loved you a lot."

Really? That was news to Nick. All he could remember about the grandfather-grandson relationship was bickering about football.

He was about to ask his father to tell him more when he heard the opening chords of Hank Williams Jr.'s Monday Night Football theme song, "Are You Ready?!"

"Ready!" he heard Coleman and Elliot bellow at the TV.

"Gotta go, Dad! See you at breakfast!"

Nick slammed down the phone and ran to join his friends. Another tradition of the Monday Night Football Club was to sing along with the opening music.

The three friends bounced wildly up and down on the couches, howling out the lyrics while windmilling invisible guitars.

Hilary pounded on the wall. "Qui-et!"

"One more broken spring," yelled Mrs. Lighter from the kitchen, "and you'll be spending your next Monday night out on the street!"

"Look!" Nick pointed excitedly at the screen. "It's going to be a close game! Dan Dierdorf's wearing the red tie!"

"Great!" Coleman agreed. "I'm glad it isn't the blue tie. That's always a blowout."

"Unless Frank Gifford has a new haircut," Elliot reminded them. "That means overtime."

It was an exciting matchup as usual, with spectacular passing, brilliant running, and bone-crushing hits. The Giants' defense kept the score close. But John Elway was unstoppable. By halftime, the Broncos led 17–10.

Mrs. Lighter poked her head into the room. "Okay, boys. Pajamas."

Pajamas at halftime was another club rule. The three friends changed and climbed into their sleeping bags to watch the rest of the game.

As usual, John Elway was the ultimate weapon. Number 7 threw for more than three hundred yards, including a touchdown pass. He even scored himself on one of his famous scrambles.

"Did you see that?" cried Nick. "He zoomed through the defense!"

"He flew into the end zone!" Elliot added breathlessly.

"He can do anything!" cheered Coleman.

"Can he make three idiots shut up and go to sleep?" called Hilary from her bedroom across the hall.

"Hilary, Hilary, Heavy Artillery," whispered Coleman.

Nick cracked up into his pillow, and Elliot reached for the nearest thing he could find to cover his laughter. It was the Eskimos jersey.

"Ugh!" he gagged when he felt the musty wool against his face. He flung the sweater away. It sailed through the air and draped itself over the top of the tall floor lamp. The lamp teetered and finally steadied. The brown uniform hung precariously over Nick's sleeping bag.

"Nice throw," Nick approved. He thrust an imaginary microphone in front of Elliot. "Please tell our audience how it feels to be the first person in history to complete the Monday Night Sleeping Bag Flying Sweater Pass to a wide receiver who's really a lamp."

"It feels great." Elliot grinned. "And now, a word from our sponsor—"

"Hey, I'm trying to hear," muttered Coleman, turning up the sound on the TV.

As the game drew on toward midnight, the Broncos mounted up a 34–17 lead. Cheers slowly turned to yawns in the Lighter living room.

Coleman was the first to fall asleep. When John Elway was replaced by his backup for the rest of the game, Nick too drifted off. Elliot stayed up to record the final yardage statistics in his notebook. As the last member awake, it was also his job to turn off the TV. Then he burrowed deep into his sleeping bag. Soon, his breathing matched the steady rhythm of his two best friends. The Monday Night Football Club was over for another week.

Had he remained awake a few minutes longer, Elliot might have witnessed something quite unusual. As Nick rolled onto his back, his leg bumped the floor lamp, jarring loose the Eskimos jersey. It dropped right on Nick's face. He began to snort and puff, trying to breathe through the heavy wool.

A moment later, a point of light appeared over the sweater. It looked almost like a firefly executing loop-the-loops.

Even if Elliot had been awake, he probably wouldn't have recognized the tiny object for what it was: a small glowing football.

And what was the strange path it traced through the air, just a few inches above the sleeping Nick? The mysterious light was writing out a number: 7.

How Ya Feeling, John?

What was this? A dream? But Nick dreamed in black and white. This was living color.

He felt water all around him. Hot, churning water, soothing his aching muscles.

A Jacuzzi? Maybe he was dreaming of his family's vacation to that resort in Puerto Rico. Any minute now, Hilary, Hilary, Heavy Artillery would go off the high diving board to impress that lifeguard, and crack her head on the side of the pool. Then the holiday would adjourn to the hospital.

But no. This wasn't vacation. He was indoors, in a small room with concrete cinder-block walls. And this was no hotel Jacuzzi. It was a metal whirlpool—the same kind sports teams used for their players.

Nick winced. His shoulder ached. Why?

His knee throbbed. And his arm stung. There may have been a tiny spot behind his left earlobe that didn't hurt. Everything else—including the roots of his hair—was killing him.

What kind of rotten dream was this?

The door swung open. In stepped a large muscular man in a tight T-shirt. He started talking. His voice was low, like he was very far away. Nick strained to listen. What was he saying?

"How ya feeling, John?"

John?!

Nick came awake with a shake to find the sweater smothering him.

"Yuck!" He pushed it away and sat up in his sleeping bag, breathing hard.

"Hey." Elliot's eyes were open. He was looking at Nick in concern. "Are you okay? You look like you've seen a ghost."

"Just a weird dream," Nick whispered. "Good night."

"Good night."

Nick lay back. His heart was pounding in his throat. The words of the man in his dream were echoing all around him. "How ya feeling, John?"

How ya feeling, *John*.

Who was John? John *Elway*?

Maybe he heard wrong. Maybe it was "How ya feeling, Ron?" Or Don, Shawn, even Deion . . .

Nick shook his head to clear it. There could be only one "John" on Nick's mind after a Broncos game. He had dreamed he was John Elway.

The problem was that it hadn't *felt* like a dream. It had felt real. Especially the aches and pains. Those had been *too* real.

Last year the Monday Night Football Club had tried a trick play called the Main Street Double-Pump Reverse Buttonhook. In it, Nick had to make the catch while riding backward on a single roller skate. He'd swerved to avoid a poodle and tripped over a fire hydrant, flying sideways to land in a pile of leaves. The Monday Night Football Club had proclaimed it his first official club injury. Well, in the whirlpool dream he had experienced the same kind of dull soreness.

His grandfather used to insist that pain was a part of football. But, of course, that wouldn't include a superstar like John Elway, would it?

Grandpa! He clutched the Eskimos sweater in his fists. Now Grandpa's kind of football was invading his sleep, thanks to this dumb old rag!

He rose to his feet and stepped over the still forms of his two friends. He opened the stereo cabinet, reached around the CD racks, and stuck the jersey behind his parents' old-style record collection.

He dusted off his hands in satisfaction. Good riddance to bad garbage. With luck, he would never have to look at that itchy, smelly, moth-eaten thing ever again!

Fifty-Three Bob, Odd Six, on One

The school bus jounced up the rutted road that led from Middletown to Overlook Outdoor Center. Class 5A bounced along, laughing, cheering, and enjoying the shaky ride. All except one student.

"When's the last time they checked the brakes on this thing?" Coleman asked nervously.

"What do you care?" Elliot laughed. "It's not your bus."

"It's a pretty steep hill!" Coleman insisted. "We could roll all the way to the bottom!"

Standing behind the driver, Mr. Sargent, the gym teacher, addressed his class. "In just a few minutes we'll be at the outdoor center. Remember, the top of the mountain is twenty degrees cooler than at school. Can anybody tell me why?"

"Because of the altitude," piped up Caitlin Mooney.

"Right," approved the teacher. "So I hope you all

remembered to bring your jackets."

"No fear," said Coleman. "You think I want to freeze to death and get pneumonia?" From his knapsack he pulled out a Gore-Tex hiker's parka with waterproof hood.

"It's a field trip, not an expedition up Mount Everest," snickered Elliot, shrugging into his own windbreaker. "Right, Nick?"

But the third member of the Monday Night Football Club didn't answer. He was staring in horror into his duffel bag. He reached in and pulled out the Eskimos jersey.

"Are you crazy?" Coleman demanded. "What did you bring that for?"

"I thought you got rid of that thing," added Elliot.

"I thought so, too," Nick replied. "I guess my mom found it and stuck it in my bag for the trip."

"You'll go nuts in that itchy sweater all afternoon," warned Elliot. "Not to mention looking like an idiot."

"And it's number 13," added Coleman.

Nick stuffed the jersey back in his bag and closed the zipper. "Maybe I won't need it."

The bus shuddered up to the outdoor center. Mr. Sargent herded Class 5A out onto the parking lot.

"Hold it right there," he said suddenly.

Nick turned around to face his teacher. "Me?"

"All right, Nick. Where's your jacket?"

"I—I'm totally comfortable," Nick stammered. A blast of wintry wind rattled the door of the bus. "I'm not that c-c-cold."

Mr. Sargent took the duffel from Nick and dumped the Eskimos jersey into his arms. "Everybody needs to dress properly, and that goes for you, too," he ordered. "When I turn around, I expect you to be in this sweater!"

As Nick struggled into the brown jersey, he flashed Coleman and Elliot a military salute. The Monday Night Football Club called the gym teacher "Sarge," and it wasn't just because of his name. Mr. Sargent could be as tough as a real marine drill sergeant—the kind who sent cadets on twenty-mile hikes.

"How do I look?" Nick demanded.

"It's not as bad as I thought," decided Elliot. "Of course, your T-shirt shows through all the holes. But maybe no one will notice."

Matthew Leopold brayed a laugh at the Monday Night Football Club. "Nice shirt!" he snickered. "Hey, Nick, did they sell *clothes* at the store where you bought it?"

Face flaming red, Nick concentrated on his sneakers. The field trip hadn't even started yet, and he was already hot, despite the blustery cold at the top of Overlook

Mountain. He had the feeling he'd be just as sweaty at the north pole.

Coleman read the compass upside down, so the Monday Night Football Club began by marching fifty paces in the wrong direction. Step two sent them squeezing through a grove of trees so dense that their faces were scratched by jagged branches and twigs. Step three would have marched them over a forty-foot cliff.

"Something's wrong," Nick decided. "Sarge is tough, but not *that* tough."

Soon they were hopelessly lost, tramping aimlessly through the woods around Overlook Outdoor Center.

"You and your number 13," accused Coleman from the depths of his Gore-Tex. "It's all your fault. I should have joined a different group."

Nick stopped in his tracks. "Haven't we passed that tree before?"

"We've passed a million trees, and they all look alike," Coleman groaned. "We're walking in circles."

Elliot checked the compass and pointed. "North is this way."

"Big deal," scoffed Coleman. "Who cares where north is? Give me a compass that always points to the bus. Now, *that* would be worth something!"

"We *could've* retraced our steps," Elliot pointed out, "if you hadn't dropped the instruction sheet down that waterfall."

Coleman sat on a stump. "Well, we can't *die*, right? That part's definite. Sarge will call the police if we don't show up at the bus by three-thirty."

Nick lay down in the soft grass beside him. "That'll be fun. Getting rescued by the cops in front of the whole class."

"Sarge'll have us court-martialed," Elliot predicted. "We'll end up cleaning the latrine with our toothbrushes."

Nick stared through the treetops at the sun, high in the afternoon sky. It was almost hypnotic. Either that or the world's itchiest sweater was making him groggy. His eyelids fluttered, then drooped.

All at once, the road map of branches faded into a different picture. It was a tight circle of faces. And a voice—a deep voice, definitely an adult. What was it saying?

"Fifty-three bob, odd six, on one!"

Whap! Elliot clapped his hands together hard, barely an inch above Nick's nose. Shocked, Nick sat up like he was on a spring-loaded trigger. He glared at Elliot. "What did you do that for?"

Elliot shrugged. "A bug was landing on your face. It

looked like a firefly." He examined his hands. "I missed it."

Nick shook his head to clear it. *Fifty-three bob, odd six, on one!* What could that mean?

Elliot stiffened like a pointer. "Hey, what's that?"

The three listened. Something was crashing through the underbrush.

Coleman looked daggers at Elliot. "You lied. You said there weren't any bears up here."

Matthew Leopold burst into the clearing. "See? I told you I heard voices! Mr. Sargent! Mr. Sargent!"

"We were better off with the bear," Elliot commented.

The teacher appeared at Matthew's side. "Just what do you guys think you're doing? Every other group has been back at the bus for half an hour already!"

"I guess we got a little lost," Nick admitted.

"Lost?" roared Mr. Sargent. "Lost means you bust your buns trying to get help! I see three lazy slackers lying around like this is Miami Beach!"

"We only stopped for a minute," Coleman defended lamely.

Matthew emitted a nasty laugh. "And you guys want to be football players? You'll be lucky if you don't flunk fifth-grade phys ed!"

Nick glowered at him. "Listen, Matthew, the stuff

we do in gym has *nothing* to do with football. You think John Elway has to hike around mountains and climb ropes and jump over vaulting horses?"

"You're way off base, Nick," snapped Mr. Sargent. "How do you think NFL players get so good?"

Nick shrugged. "Because of their talent."

The teacher shook his head. "Because they work hard. Do you know the kind of shape you have to be in just to *run* with those guys? If you're going to have a prayer of making it to the NFL, the first thing that has to change is your lazy attitude!" He reached out a hand and hauled Nick to his feet. "Now, let's go. The others are waiting."

There was a whole lot of saluting on the walk back to the bus. Matthew tried to tattle, but Mr. Sargent silenced him with a look that would have melted lead.

"You think Sarge could be right?" whispered Coleman, puffing to keep up with the teacher's long strides.

"Yeah, sure," Nick replied sarcastically. "I can just picture John Elway preparing for a big game by getting lost in the woods." He snorted. "Sarge talks just like my grandpa used to: 'hard work, dedication, sacrifice.' It's all hot air."

* * * *

Nick never watched the evening news. But on Wednesdays, he always joined his mother and Hilary in front of the TV for the *Sport Report*. It was the day the experts previewed the next week's NFL action.

Nick couldn't believe his good fortune. The Broncos were playing on *Monday Night Football* for the second week in a row. This almost never happened. One thing would be different, though. Denver was the home team, hosting the Dallas Cowboys.

"Was he hatched, or did we find him somewhere?" asked Hilary. "He couldn't care less about world peace, the president, and the United Nations, but now that they're talking about football, he's glued to the screen."

"He gets it from Grandpa," laughed Mrs. Lighter.

"Shhh!" Nick complained. "I'm trying to watch this!"

The broadcast included an actual videotape of the Broncos' practice that afternoon. It was amazing! There was John Elway, Terrell Davis, Shannon Sharpe—the cameraman was so close to the huddle that you could even hear Elway calling the play.

"Fifty-three bob, odd six, on one!"

What?!

That was it! The strange sentence from his daydream at Overlook Outdoor Center!

He thought back. He remembered a circle of faces. The Broncos' huddle!

But . . . but . . .

He pulled his knees in to his chest, breathing hard. It wasn't so bizarre that he was imagining the Denver huddle. But how could he know their play calling? Their code words? Stuff like that had to be secret for any football team, let alone one of the top offenses in the NFL!

His sister's voice brought him back to earth. "Mom, I think something's wrong with the doofus. He looks like he has a fever."

Mrs. Lighter put her hand on Nick's forehead. "You're not warm, but you look very pale. And you've been acting kind of scatterbrained lately."

"Scatterbrained?" Nick repeated. "Come on, Mom. What am I, a five-year-old?"

"But it's true," she insisted. "Just this afternoon, I found your grandfather's football jersey wadded up in the bottom of the garbage can. That's the second time I've had to rescue that sweater, Nicky. I know how heartbroken you'd be if you lost it. Are you sure everything's all right?"

Oh, A-OK, fine and dandy, Mom. This afternoon I heard the secret play call from some famous superstars in a football practice two thousand miles away. What could be wrong with that?

Of course, a guy couldn't say these things to his mother. Personal business this important could only be revealed to the Monday Night Football Club!

The Weisbaum Broken-Field
Lateral Tree Punt

"Maybe you remembered it wrong," was Coleman's opinion the next day at morning recess.

"No way," Nick insisted. "I know what I heard—first at the outdoor center, and then on TV in the Broncos' huddle. How weird is that?"

"You must have fallen asleep for a split second in the woods," Elliot reasoned. "So you dreamed about the huddle. Big deal."

"But what about their play call?" Nick persisted. "How could I dream it if I don't know it?"

"Well," Elliot mused thoughtfully, "in science they say your dreaming mind can know stuff that your awake mind doesn't."

Coleman looked startled. "Really? Maybe my dreaming mind might have known the answers on that history test I flunked. I should sleep in class more often."

"Be serious!" Nick growled. "Don't forget—this comes on top of that crazy dream where I was in the whirlpool and that guy called me John."

"Maybe you're going nuts," Coleman offered help- fully.

"Thanks," Nick groaned. "That makes me feel a lot better."

"Look," said Elliot, "you're the biggest football fan in the world. You even have the same initials as the league. You eat, breathe, and sleep football. So now you're dreaming it, too. So what?"

"And the play call?"

Elliot shrugged. "Maybe Elway called an audible once, and you heard it over the TV. Who knows what we could remember deep down? Don't look for mysteries where there are none. Now quit sulking, and let's work on the Weisbaum Broken-Field Lateral Tree Punt."

The new trick play was one of the most difficult they had ever attempted. The idea had been born when Elliot noticed that Miss Weisbaum kept all the windows of her portable classroom wide open. The maneuver began with Nick passing the ball through Miss Weisbaum's room—in one window and out the other—to Elliot on the south side of the portable. Elliot would then run the entire length of the primary playground, right through the first-grade jump ropes. Then he would lateral the ball to Coleman. It was Coleman's job to punt the football into the elm tree by the parking lot.

"But it has to stay up in the branches," Elliot finished. "If it falls out, the play doesn't count."

The three members of the Monday Night Football Club took their positions. Nick was the quarterback.

"Hut, hut, *hike!*"

He took careful aim and threw. The ball sizzled into the classroom, over the computer, past the glass lizard habitat, and out the opposite window.

Elliot was right there. He snatched the ball out of the air, tucked it under his arm, and took off.

"Go, man!" cried Nick, running out from behind the portable for a better view.

Elliot swung around a hopscotch game and leaped over two third-graders trading hockey cards. He was going full steam by the time he reached the first jump rope.

"Gangway!" he bellowed.

The twirling rope missed him by inches. He danced through off-balance and stumbled into the second rope, stiff with panic.

"Duck!" howled Nick.

Elliot tucked his head into his neck, skipped twice, and escaped the spiraling rope, still on his feet. He headed for the parking lot amid a shower of insults from the first-grade girls.

As Elliot crossed the playground, Coleman came sprinting in from the softball diamond. The two ran side by side. Then Elliot flipped the ball into Coleman's sure hands.

Without missing a step, Coleman punted the ball with all his might. The kick sailed high, a perfect spiral through the air. It landed dead center in the elm tree. The ball trembled for a breathless moment, and settled. There it sat, wedged in the crook of a delicate branch.

Nick came racing up behind them. He thrust his imaginary microphone over Coleman's shoulder and into his face. "Tell the folks at home how it felt to make the greatest kick in the history of football!"

"Well—," Coleman began.

Before he could continue the "interview," a large crow landed in the tree. It approached the ball, flapping and squawking.

"Hey, cut that out!" cried Coleman in dismay.

But the bird hopped closer. Cautiously, it pecked the ball. Then it grew bolder. It began to nudge and push this strange object that had invaded its home.

"*No-o!*" chorused the Monday Night Football Club in agony.

The football teetered once and toppled out of the tree. It bounced off the hood of the principal's car, and came to rest at their feet.

"It's a do-over," said Nick sadly.

"No fair!" moaned Coleman. "It would still be up there if it wasn't for that stupid bird!"

Elliot shook his head. "NFL rules."

"NFL rules?" Coleman repeated. "They don't have the Weisbaum Broken-Field Lateral Tree Punt in the NFL! How can there be a rule about it?"

"If a pass bounces off the referee," Elliot explained, "it's still a live ball."

"But at least the ref is a person!" Coleman argued. "This is a *crow*! He's not even wearing a striped shirt!"

"But he counts as part of the play," Nick said patiently. "Take my word for it. It's a do-over."

So they got back into position for their second try at the Weisbaum Broken-Field Lateral Tree Punt.

"Hut, hut, *hike!*"

The ball sailed through the portable and thumped into Elliot's chest. He hugged it tightly and started off toward the skipping ropes.

"Look out! It's him again!" shrieked one girl, diving out of Elliot's path.

He made it through the first rope and bounded on.

"Oh, no!" he cried when he saw the second group. They were now skipping double Dutch.

One rope wound around his neck. The other tripped him at the ankles.

Wham!

"Should I go get the nurse?" Coleman called anxiously.

"Why?" groaned Elliot. "Does she moonlight as a gravedigger?"

"Hurry up! Get back in the huddle!" Nick shouted. "We're in time pressure!"

It was true. Recess was almost over.

Elliot joined them. "Okay," he gasped. "We've got one more chance to make this."

Coleman nodded. "And whoever messes up dies."

Nick had to laugh. "Big talk from a guy who faints every time his mom has to pull a splinter out of his pinkie."

"Hey, man," Coleman protested. "I can take any punishment you can."

"Okay," said Elliot, "how about the guy who messes up has to miss *Monday Night Football*?"

"Don't be an idiot!" snapped Nick. "That could never happen. How about this: if it's your fault, you have to eat a jar of Luigi's Volcano-Hot Mustard."

"That's not fair," objected Coleman. "I have a weak stomach."

"I've got it!" Elliot exclaimed. "If you blow the play, you have to wear Nick's grandfather's sweater for an entire Monday Night Football Club."

Nick laughed. "Settle for the mustard. I've worn that thing. You guys don't know what you're getting into."

"Deal," said Coleman. "Goat wears the shirt. Get in position."

Nick checked his watch. Thirty seconds to the bell. He was so focused on getting a good grip on the football that he didn't notice Miss Weisbaum returning to her classroom.

"Oh, it looks like rain," the teacher commented. "I'd better close these windows."

"Ready!" called Elliot from the other side of the portable.

"Hut, hut, *hike!*"

Nick wound up and fired. He saw the closed window a millionth of a second after the ball left his hand.

Crash! Tinkle!

Miss Weisbaum screamed in shock; students came running; teachers began to appear from everywhere.

Coleman and Elliot looked at Nick as if they'd never seen him before in their lives, and they melted into the crowd. The bell rang.

"Nicholas Lighter," called the principal from his office window. "I'll see you immediately, please."

And in the midst of this chaos, there was only one thought in Nick's mind: he had to spend his treasured Monday night suffering the misery of Grandpa's awful shirt.

Kings of the Castle

Nick emptied a bag of fresh sand into the lizard habitat in Miss Weisbaum's classroom. He placed a handful of stones artistically around the surface.

"All done, Miss Weisbaum," he called. It was Monday, and day three of his week of detentions for breaking the window of the portable.

The teacher appeared, lugging a large Tupperware bowl. Inside, two pale green gecko lizards darted around nervously. "Romeo and Juliet haven't been very happy since your trick play smashed their old home," she commented.

"Sorry," he murmured. When was he *ever* going to be allowed to stop apologizing for the broken window, the busted bowl, the sand and glass on the floor—*and* the countless scrapes and bruises suffered by twenty-four third-graders as they raced about trying to catch Romeo and Juliet?

Miss Weisbaum released the lizards into their new terrarium. "Oh, they're much happier now."

Nick wasn't paying attention. He was staring out into the school yard. There, Coleman and Elliot jumped up and down, waving their arms and making faces.

Frantically, he signaled for them to go away. They jumped higher and waved harder.

Miss Weisbaum sighed. "You know, Nick, we teachers aren't as stupid or as blind as you fifth-graders seem to think. I assume those two are the other part of your trick play."

Nick looked shocked. "How did you know?"

The teacher smiled. "Nobody passes a football with a lizard as the intended receiver." She placed the glass lid over Romeo and Juliet. "Go and join your friends. I'll see you tomorrow at three-thirty."

Nick ran out of the portable. Coleman and Elliot greeted him, still making faces.

"Thanks for waiting, guys."

"Oh, we didn't wait." Coleman tossed Nick his sleeping bag. "We just got back. We stopped by your place to pick up the sweater."

Nick's face fell. He had been hoping that his friends might have forgotten his penalty for messing up the Weisbaum Broken-Field Lateral Tree Punt.

* * * *

The Galloway home had the best Monday Night Football Club setup in the group—an attic room where the guys could spread out their sleeping bags and not be disturbed.

"But you've got to watch out," Coleman reminded them. He patted the sloping walls. "You could bash in your head."

"It's worth it," Elliot decided. "Up here, we're the kings of the castle. We have total privacy."

With that, there was the clatter of small feet. Up out of the stairwell appeared the round grinning face of Coleman's little brother, Jeffrey.

"Hey, everybody!" Jeffrey's voice would have shattered glass. "Guess what?"

Coleman stared at him in horror. "What are *you* doing here? I thought you were staying over at Ari's tonight."

"Ari has the mumps," the seven-year-old announced cheerfully. "So I'm allowed to be in the Monday Night Football Club with you guys."

Coleman threw back his head and bellowed, "Mo-o-om!"

Soon there was the clicking of high heels on the stairs. Mrs. Galloway's head poked up beside Jeffrey's.

"Yes, I know," she said before Coleman could launch

into his complaint. "But have a heart, Coleman. Jeffrey is so disappointed that his sleepover had to be canceled."

"Then let him go and catch the mumps from Ari!" howled Coleman. "He looks like a chipmunk already with those puffy cheeks!"

"Apologize to your little brother, young man!"

But the dam had burst, and Coleman couldn't hold back the flood waters. "I only care about one thing in the whole world—Monday night! All I want is to enjoy it in peace! Do I ever ask for anything else?"

"Frequently," his mother replied drily. "You ask for HBO, Rollerblades, Super-Nintendo, a raise in your allowance, a motorcycle—"

"I mean, besides that stuff!" Coleman blustered.

Mrs. Galloway addressed Nick and Elliot. "You boys don't mind, do you?"

The two exchanged agonized glances. Mind? No more than they'd mind a tornado roaring through the attic. "It's okay, Mrs. Galloway," they chorused in resignation.

"Okay?!" Coleman raged. "It's not okay! It isn't even close to okay!"

"Besides," Mrs. Galloway whispered behind her hand, "Jeffrey will be asleep long before kickoff. You won't even know he's here."

"Oh, boy," Jeffrey squealed as his mother clicked away. "This is going to be so cool!"

"It's not going to be that cool," Elliot sighed.

"We have to do our homework before game time," Coleman told his brother. "So scram."

"I've got homework, too!" Jeffrey burbled. "I know— I'll do it with you guys!" He sprinted downstairs and returned a moment later with a pack of times-tables flash cards.

As the Monday Night Football Club struggled to get their studying done, Jeffrey bounced around the attic like a Ping-Pong ball, bellowing, "Five times five— *twenty-five!*"

Coleman looked so down in the dumps that Nick gave him a friendly punch on the arm. "Hey, man. We've all got brothers and sisters. They're like bad weather— they stink, but what can you do about it?"

"You can move to Florida," Coleman said sulkily.

"Seven times three—*twenty-one!*" shrieked Jeffrey.

Elliot frowned. "Are you sure about that? I think it's actually thirty-four."

Jeffrey turned the card over. "Nope. Twenty-one. See? It says so right here."

Elliot pointed to the trademark on the back. "Look at this: 'Printed in Japan.' Japanese math is different from ours. In America, seven times three is thirty-four."

The second-grader looked worried. "You mean these cards are all wrong?"

Elliot flashed a wink at Nick and Coleman. "Just the ones with sevens in them. Japanese math is the same as ours if there are no sevens. So seven times four is forty-six. Seven times five is eighty. And seven times seven is nine hundred. Have you got a pen? I can change these for you."

"Great," muttered Coleman. "Now he's going to flunk math, and I'm going to have to tutor him—probably on Monday nights."

"What an ugly sweater!" shrilled Jeffrey over pizza. "How come you're wearing such an ugly sweater?"

"It's a long story," sighed Nick. He toyed with the idea of convincing the kid that it was a big privilege to wear Grandpa's instrument of torture. But Coleman and Elliot would never let him get away with it. Anyway, he was too exhausted to try.

The past few days had been tough on Nick. It wasn't just because of his detention. He had never really gotten over his vision of the Broncos' huddle. Every night he lay awake, trying to tell himself that it had been just a coincidence. But nothing could change the fact that he had daydreamed a play that he could not possibly have known about. It was weird, and maybe a little bit creepy, too.

Hilary, Hilary, Heavy Artillery wasn't making it any easier for her brother to sleep. On Friday, she had bought the world's loudest rap record. Even on low volume, the bass rattled every window in the house.

Nick yawned.

Coleman looked at him in concern. "What are you—tired? On Monday night? Are you crazy?"

"I'm not tired at all," piped up Jeffrey. "I'm going to stay up for the whole game. I'm going to pull an all-nighter."

For Nick, his grandfather's shirt was the icing on the hot and itchy cake. He'd tried to hide it, and even throw it out. Each time it had come back to find him.

That heavy wool was meant to keep the Minnesota cold off the North Brainerd Eskimos. Indoors, it could put a wildcat to sleep. *Monday Night Football* hadn't even started yet, and he could already feel his eyelids drooping . . . drooping . . .

I'm John Elway

The roar of the crowd was deafening. Nick looked up. Thousands—no, *tens* of thousands of screaming, waving, cheering people. He wheeled. More people. They were all around him!

Somewhere, a whistle blew—

Jeffrey Galloway's eyes lit up. He stared at the tiny glowing football that danced above Nick's sleeping form.

"Hey, a firefly!" He lunged forward to try to catch it in his hands. His foot came down hard right on Nick's stomach.

"Oof!" Nick's body jackknifed straight up into the air. He came awake, dazed. "What . . . what . . . where did all the people go?"

"Take it easy," Elliot soothed. "You dozed off."

"It isn't even nine o'clock yet," added Coleman. "Are you sick or something?"

"Just tired," Nick yawned. "This sweater is killing me."

Jeffrey peeked inside his cupped palms. No firefly. "Darn it, I missed him." He looked around. "Where did he go?"

Elliot unrolled his sleeping bag on the floor in front of the TV. "Since you're being such a wimp about it, Nick, go ahead—take off the jersey. We don't want to ruin your life."

"Right," Coleman confirmed. "So what if it breaks the rules of the club? So what if we never respect you again? So what if—"

"I'll wear the dumb sweater!" Nick exploded.

Jeffrey ran for the stairs. "There's a firefly in here somewhere!" he exclaimed. "I'm going to get a jar so I can catch him!"

"Don't hurry back," snarled Coleman.

The clock struck nine, and *Monday Night Football* burst onto the television screen. The three friends added their own sound effects as Frank Gifford hyped the game to come. And when Hank Williams Jr. appeared for the opening music, the three chorused, *"Are you ready for some footba-a-all?"*

Another meeting of the Monday Night Football Club was in full swing.

Nick found it hard to dance and sing his way through the theme song. He couldn't believe he was dozing and dreaming again—during the greatest three hours of the week! For the past four days, he had hardly been able to sleep at all. And now fate was pulling a reverse on him—at nine o'clock on Monday night! It just wasn't fair.

He lay back down on his sleeping bag and tried to focus on the screen. John Elway was jogging out onto the field. Nick's eyelids felt like they weighed a hundred pounds each.

Now he couldn't even stay awake for John Elway! Oh, no! What was going . . . on . . . here . . . ? Once more, he dropped off to sleep.

"Well, what do you know," Elliot commented absently. "Your kid brother was right. There *is* a firefly in here."

The snap thumped into Nick's chest, leaving his breast-bone stinging.

"Ow!" *Who could hike a ball that hard? Coleman? Elliot?*

He wheeled on his cleats—*cleats?*—and tucked the ball under his arm.

Why am I in the middle of a football game?

The ground under him shook with the pounding of thundering feet. Nick's eyes darted all around. Defenders were coming at him from everywhere—*huge* people who could run like gazelles! Nick panicked. He'd be crushed like a bug!

His fear must have added wings to his feet. He scrambled away from the stampede.

I'm dreaming, Nick thought to himself. *No way I can run this fast.*

Suddenly, a linebacker came out of nowhere and lunged at Nick. Nick felt arms like the jaws of a bear trap clamp around his waist.

I'm dead! shot through his mind.

Before the thought even reached his brain, his body snapped into action. He swiveled a hip, stopped on a dime, and whirled ballet-style away from the tackle.

Holy Toledo, how did I do that?

His eyes zoomed in on the open receiver. His arm cocked back, and fired.

But I can't throw that far!

The pass took off like a bazooka rocket. It sizzled over the defense and into the end zone where it struck the receiver right between the numbers. The referee— *referee?!*—raised both arms.

"Touchdown!"

The roar of the crowd was louder than anything Nick could have imagined. Yes, it was the same crowd he'd seen before. It wasn't a dream; all this was *real!* But how?

A teammate came running over and awarded him a mighty slap on the back. "Great pass!"

Nick gawked at the famous face in the football helmet before him. It was Terrell Davis, the star running back of the Denver Broncos.

"What are you doing here?" Nick blurted, flabbergasted.

Has my voice gotten deeper? he asked himself.

The well-known features relaxed into an amused grin. "I work here," Davis laughed. "Don't you?"

For the first time, Nick noticed that he too was wearing a Broncos' uniform. He looked down at the front of his own jersey.

His heart skipped a beat. The number was 7. It was impossible, and yet it was happening here in real life!

I can't believe it! he thought. *I'm John Elway!*

The Bug House

Jeffrey Galloway struggled up the attic stairs with an enormous carton. At the top, he set it down and dragged it over to Nick's sleeping form. Inside the box, jars and bottles clinked.

Coleman tore his eyes away from the game. "Oh, no, you don't! Not the bug house! Not now!"

"It's not a bug house; it's my insect collection," said Jeffrey cheerfully. "I brought a jar for the firefly. Have you seen him?"

"I think he was going to California," put in Elliot, concentrating on a penalty call. "If you hurry, you can catch up."

Jeffrey sat down and began removing jars from the carton. "Here's my daddy longlegs. And here's the tick; it's really small. I had sixty ants in this one, but some of them died. I keep moths in here, cater-pillars in the pickle jar, and—oh, yeah, here's the best of all—two praying mantises."

"I'll bet I know what they're praying for," said Coleman through clenched teeth. "They want you to shut up."

"You're not allowed to be mean to me!" Jeffrey bellowed indignantly.

The sleeping figure of Nick rolled over onto his side but didn't wake. He snored just a little. "Is the warm-up over yet, Coach?" he mumbled. "I can't find my helmet."

Jeffrey laughed triumphantly. "Hah! Mom said *I* wouldn't make it to the kickoff. One of *you* guys is sleeping, and *I'm* still awake!"

Elliot shook his head. "You know, Nick is going to kill himself for missing this one. Elway's having his best game all season."

Coleman nodded in agreement. "Elway's awesome."

"Thanks," came a drowsy murmur from the depths of Nick's sleeping bag.

The Denver Broncos' bench was a crazy place. Everyone seemed to be yelling at the same time. Messages were sent and received through headsets and over phone lines. Hand signals flashed on and off the field. Trainers taped and retaped ankles and knees. Coaches diagrammed plays on mini-chalkboards.

Head Coach Mike Shanahan was the nerve center. All information began and ended with him. And it was his voice that was heard above the others, even over the loudest cheering of the crowd.

Nick sat on the bench, vibrating with excitement. Talk about a dream coming true! How many times had he prayed to go to an NFL game even if he had to sit in the worst seat in the stadium—last row, higher up than the Goodyear blimp, behind a post, in the pouring rain. Now he was *on the field*—not just watching, but a part of it all!

Everything about the NFL was larger than life. The players were humongous.

I'm not so small myself, Nick thought, looking down at John Elway's long legs.

Even the Gatorade bucket seemed enormous here. You could float a battleship in all that liquid. Nobody could finish it in a thousand years. Yet his teammates were putting away gallons of the stuff.

He got up to have a drink and was astonished when he slugged back an entire quart. Nick Lighter couldn't drink that much. But apparently John Elway was a thirsty guy.

"Let's go, John!" barked Coach Shanahan. "First down!"

Nick jogged out onto the field, scared stiff. How was he going to know the play? Sure, he had John Elway's body. But that wouldn't do any good if his passes were all twenty yards away from their receivers. How would he know where to *throw*?

Then something strange and wonderful happened. The play to call came over his helmet headset: "Eighteen cross, slant four, on one!"

And Nick *knew*. His assignment appeared in his mind as clear as a road map.

In Elway's mind, he reminded himself.

"Hut!"

Quick snap; quick step; quick throw to tight end Shannon Sharpe.

One first down, coming up. Nick celebrated.

Pow! The linebacker hit him a split second after he released the ball. He crashed heavily to the grass.

The collision knocked the wind out of him, but he hardly noticed. "This is even more exciting than on TV!" he croaked to Sharpe in the huddle. "Right, Mr. Sharpe?"

The superstar gave him a funny look. "You sure you're feeling okay, John?"

"Better than I've ever felt!"

The next play called for a fake handoff. He held the

ball out to Terrell Davis, then Nick quickly covered it up in his arms.

The Dallas safeties took the bait. They sprang forward to stop the run—leaving the Broncos' receivers uncovered!

Oh no! Tony Tolbert, the defensive end, was coming at him like a charging rhino.

What do I do now? Nick thought desperately. But Elway's instincts snapped him into action.

He pumped his arm, but didn't throw. Tolbert leaped to block the "pass," and Nick did a quick spin move around him.

An Elway Special!

He reared back and hurled the ball to a streaking Ed McCaffrey. The perfect pass dropped right into McCaffrey's outstretched arms in the end zone.

"Touchdown!"

Suddenly, Nick felt himself leaping high in the air. Every time he touched the ground, his powerful legs would launch him up again.

What's going on here? he thought in alarm. Why was his body moving without him?

Now his arms were going too, pumping above his head.

It hit Nick like a bolt of lightning.

It's the celebration! I'm doing John Elway's famous touchdown celebration!

If Coleman and Elliot could see him now! If his family could!

Well, maybe not Grandpa. This was exactly the kind of thing his grandfather had never understood. But Nick did.

When you make a big play, the energy fills you up like a balloon. The celebration is how you let it all out.

At that moment, Nick was happier than he had ever been in his life!

John Elway Blows His Nose

The Broncos were playing their usual strong game. But the Dallas quarterback was the legendary Troy Aikman. Just before the two-minute warning, Aikman completed a forty-yard touchdown pass to Michael Irvin. When the gun went off at halftime, the Broncos trailed the Cowboys 14–10. Nick and his teammates were disappointed but determined to come back in the second half.

They marched through the cement tunnel that led to the locker room. The clatter of cleats against the concrete floor was just about the purest football sound Nick could have imagined. He did a mini tap-dance as he walked, straining to separate his own *clackety-clack* from the other Broncos.

The parade of orange jerseys turned left into the locker room. But Nick was so focused on his cleats that kept going straight down the tunnel. *Clack! Clack!* echoed in the silence.

Silence?

Hold it! Hold everything! Where did everybody go?

Nick spun in circles, searching for his teammates. He was alone. Oh, no! He was lost in the guts of Mile High Stadium! His only chance to ever get inside a real NFL locker room and he was *missing* it!

He tried to retrace his steps. All the doors looked the same.

Pick the wrong one, and you'll wander out at some hot dog stand. The great John Elway will look like a total idiot.

Breathing a silent prayer he threw open a door . . .

And he found himself staring into the face of a football legend—Lynn Swann, the Hall of Fame receiver who did interviews for *Monday Night Football*.

"The locker room!" Nick blurted. "Where's the locker room?"

Bewildered, Swann pointed.

"Thanks!"

Nick rushed off, kicking himself. What a wasted opportunity. A chance to talk with a real Hall of Famer! Coleman and Elliot would never let him hear the end of it.

He stopped, frowning. *Those guys probably won't believe this crazy stuff anyway,* he reflected. *I barely believe it myself.*

He turned back to the *Monday Night Football*

reporter. "Hey, Mr. Swann, can I send a message to Al Michaels in the broadcast booth?"

"We'll get to the highlights in just a minute," Al Michaels was saying on the TV in Coleman's attic. "But first, I have a request from John Elway in the Broncos' locker room."

"Hey, check it out." Elliot turned up the volume on the set.

"John asked me to send out a special hello," the play-by-play announcer went on, "to his good friends Coleman and Elliot in the Monday Night Football Club."

"What?!" The two sat bolt upright in their sleeping bags.

"How would John Elway know about *us*?" Elliot gaped.

"He must have read my fan letter!" Coleman cheered. "This is the coolest night of my life! I can't believe Nick's missing it!"

"But Elway must get millions of letters," Elliot protested. "Why would he focus on us over everybody else?"

"Is that John Elway?" piped up Jeffrey, pointing to Frank Gifford.

"It figures," snorted Coleman. "You say you're in the Monday Night Football Club, but you don't even know John Elway."

"I'm here," came a dreamy mumble beside him. Nick's sleeping bag stretched and settled as its occupant rolled over.

Coleman stared. A small beetle was crawling along the shoulder of the Eskimos sweater. "Watch it," he told his brother. "Some of your stupid bugs are getting loose."

"I'm *exercising* them," Jeffrey explained. "The caterpillar's next. He needs to be really healthy so he can spin a cocoon and turn into a butterfly."

"Yeah, well, Nick isn't a jogging track," warned Coleman.

"Hey," said Elliot. "Elway left out Nick. He said hi to you and me, but he forgot his biggest fan of all."

"Maybe Nick's letter got lost in the mail," Coleman suggested.

"Yeah, maybe." But Elliot looked puzzled. Why would Elway forget Nick? More important, why would John Elway be sending his greeting at all?

Nick stared at the small mirror in the back of the locker. Elway's face stared back at him.

That's not me! It can't be me!

Experimentally, he winked. In the mirror, Elway winked back. He stuck out his tongue; Elway stuck out his. He thumbed his nose; Elway gave it right back to him.

"Quit fooling around, John," snapped Coach Shanahan. "This is a big game."

Now the superstar's reflection looked embarrassed. There was no getting away from it. The mirror didn't lie. He was John Elway, and this was his face.

He examined his hero's locker. His eyes wandered over Elway's spare uniforms and pads. He felt slightly guilty—like when he and Coleman and Elliot rifled through Hilary's closet looking for teen magazines and love notes and good blackmail stuff.

But these are your own things, he reminded himself. *You're John Elway.*

A box of Kleenex sat on the small shelf. *John Elway blows his nose! He's human!* He tried, unsuccessfully, to picture it in his mind.

In a lot of ways, the great Captain Comeback was a pretty normal guy. His pencil had teeth marks on it, just like Nick's at school. His locker was even kind of messy, with a cell phone, cologne, dental floss, a shoehorn, sunglasses, and all kinds of assorted junk jumbled in with the equipment. Taped to the inside of the door was a birthday card. Nick flipped it open. Inside was written: *Happy Birthday to a wonderful son! Love, Mom and Dad.*

John Elway had parents!

At the bottom was scribbled, *PS: When the blitz*

comes, double pump to freeze the pass rush—Dad.

Of course! Elway's father was a successful football coach. It made sense that he would give pointers to his son—just like Mr. and Mrs. Lighter helped Nick with homework and sports and stuff.

But I just used that move on Tony Tolbert! he thought in wonder. I can do whatever Elway can.

Nick pulled out a thick notebook and flipped through the pages. Complex diagrams of *X*s and *O*s jumped out at him.

It was the Denver Broncos' playbook! The brainpower behind one of the best teams in football! Nick cradled it reverently in his hands like he was holding delicate crystal.

Nick stared. Every play had complicated formations, blocking, and patterns run by the backs and receivers. Each of the eleven positions had an important assignment. There were outs and slants, play-action passes and delays, reverses and long bombs. He flipped ahead to the dozens of defensive formations. Then came the special teams' plays. Hundreds and hundreds of diagrams covered every possible game situation!

Nick looked in wonder around the locker room at his teammates. How did these guys remember all that stuff? You had to be a genius! It was like a math class where you needed to know the whole textbook for every single quiz! How did they do it?

The answer came from something Nick's grandfather always used to say: "In football, you spend more time studying than tackling." Well, Grandpa sure was right about that! And the quarterback had to know everybody's job inside out. That meant nobody studied harder than John Elway!

As Coach Shanahan launched into his pep talk for the second half, one of the trainers walked by Nick. *Hey*, Nick realized. *I know that man!*

He snapped his fingers. It was the trainer from the whirlpool dream last Monday night. The man who had called him John. Only—how could he dream about a *real* guy he didn't even know existed?

Unless it hadn't been a dream at all! Maybe last week, like tonight, he was starting to become John Elway. But because the Eskimos shirt was lying on his face suffocating him, he'd awakened before the change could be completed.

It all made sense! The incident at Overlook Outdoor Center was exactly the same thing. He didn't *daydream* the huddle at the Broncos' practice. He was *there* in John Elway's body. And he probably would have stayed Elway if Elliot hadn't awakened him by clapping at that firefly.

The adult voice that called the play had been *him*!

And tonight nothing had woken him up before the transfer had taken place. So now he was John Elway until . . .

When?

"What's the matter, John?" asked the trainer. "You don't look so hot."

"I'm okay." Nick looked at the practice schedule taped to the inside of his playbook. He gawked. It told of a grueling week of two-a-day workouts, weight training, and three-hour team meetings to watch game films.

"Wait a minute," Nick said to the trainer. "I don't have to do all this, do I?"

The man stared at him. "What are you talking about?"

"I'm John Elway," Nick explained. "I give interviews. I sign autographs. I star in television commercials. I don't have time for all this."

"But you're the biggest workout maniac on the team!" protested the trainer.

"I *am*?"

As Nick stood gaping, Shannon Sharpe clapped him on the shoulder. "You missed a great barbecue at my place, John."

"Why . . . why couldn't I go?" Nick stammered.

The tight end laughed. "You couldn't pass up your

ten-mile run. Man, you've got to give yourself a rest!"

Ten-mile runs! Two-a-day workouts! Memorizing a hundred-page playbook! Soaking your aches and pains in a whirlpool!

That sounded like . . . Grandpa's kind of football!

It hit Nick like a ton of bricks. He'd always thought John Elway was so great that he didn't have to work hard. The truth was that Elway was great *because* he worked hard!

Elway's football and Grandpa's football were exactly the same thing!

11

The Nearest Thing to Flying

"Hut!"

The snap stung Nick's hands. This time, the Cowboys' defense wouldn't bite on the play-action fake. He dropped back, scanning the field. Nobody was open.

The two lines battled it out, and big bodies started to go down. He felt a brief moment of panic. All those hulking speeding monsters had one target—Nick Lighter.

I'm going to end up a tiny grease spot on the twenty-yard line!

Then his feet began to move as though they had a mind of their own, and he remembered.

I'm John Elway, one of the best scrambling quarterbacks in NFL history!

As he tucked away the ball, he felt a surge of energy. He could sense Elway's thousands of hours of workouts and training in every single step.

Crunch!

Terrell Davis knocked down the Dallas nose tackle. Elway's built-in radar zeroed in on the hole in the Cowboys' line. By the time the thought reached Nick's head, Elway's body was already barreling through the gap. He bounced off one tackler, hurdled the out-stretched arms of another, then steamrolled right over a third. A glorious sight met his eyes. There, sixty yards distant, was the goal line. And there were no white jerseys in the way.

It wasn't flying, but it was the nearest thing to it. Nick revved up Elway's legs like a racing driver testing a new Formula One car. The run was so fast that he could actually feel wind in his face. The roar of the crowd spurred him to even greater speed. He burst into the end zone like he'd been shot from a cannon. Touchdown! Denver was back in the lead!

The excitement was too much for Nick. He reared back and hurled the ball into the upper deck. Maybe some kid like Nick Lighter would go home tonight with a fantastic souvenir—a touchdown ball from John Elway.

In the Galloway attic, Coleman and Elliot were jumping up and down, exchanging high fives.

"Careful!" Jeffrey warned. "If you step on my lady-bug, I'm telling!"

"Did you *see* that?" crowed Elliot. "What a run!"

"Awesome," Coleman agreed. "And how'd you like to be the lucky fan who gets that ball?"

On TV, the *Monday Night Football* cameras zoomed in on a solitary spectator in the upper deck of Mile High Stadium. The touchdown football sat in the wreckage of his extra-large milk shake. His glasses were frosted and oozing, and thick chocolate malt dripped from his hair, his eyebrows, his mustache, and his shirt.

"That's probably not what John had in mind," chortled Dan Dierdorf. The commentators had a good laugh at the unfortunate fan's expense.

"What happened?" Jeffrey complained. "Why is that man all brown?"

Elliot was weak with laughter. "Elway threw the ball into the stands, and that guy got it right in the milk shake!"

"Oops . . . sorry . . . ," came a faint murmur from under Nick's pillow.

The fourth quarter was crunch time on *Monday Night Football*. Both defenses dug in. The game became a battle of running backs and punters. The line of scrimmage moved up and down the field, but neither team scored.

Nick realized that this was just another part of what

it took to play in the NFL—mental toughness in a close grinding game.

The crowd grew quieter, and so did the bench. Backed up inside their own five-yard-line, Denver was forced to punt. Nick could taste the frustration as the offense jogged off the field.

Guard Mark Schlereth nudged him with an arm the size of a telephone pole. "Those Dallas linemen are like redwoods!" he gasped. "You can't move them an inch!"

Nick nodded. It sure was tough to hang onto a three-point advantage. It reminded him of something his grandfather used to say. "Holding a lead is like being a lion tamer," he quoted aloud. "You only get one mistake."

"Who said that?" laughed the big man.

"Raymond Lighter," Nick replied.

"There's a guy who knows his football."

"I didn't think so at first," agreed Nick. "But I'm sure of it now."

He smiled at the rock-solid veteran. The Broncos were more than just great athletes. They were really nice people, too. Of course, they might not be so welcoming if they knew he was an eleven-year-old kid from Middletown, and not John Elway at all.

But he *was* Elway now. It was the greatest thing that

had ever happened. A total miracle! Why, when he told Coleman and Elliot—

But *how* could he tell them? He could show up in a limo, but the guys wouldn't see their old pal Nick; they'd see John Elway. They'd ask for his autograph. They sure wouldn't believe that he was really their friend and classmate. They might not even invite him to take part in the trick play of the week, even though he'd be really great at it now that he was big and fast and talented.

And he'd never be able to explain all this to his family. Who could expect Mom and Dad to believe that this tall football star was their little Nicky? And even though, at six feet three, he wouldn't have to take any guff from Hilary, Hilary, Heavy Artillery, he was pretty sure he'd miss her.

His heart clutched at some hope. Maybe this wasn't permanent. Maybe he could go back to his old self. Being John Elway was something he would always treasure, but Nick had family, friends, a life. Plus Elway was in his thirties, and Nick Lighter was eleven. He'd lose all the years in between. That was a lot of important stuff— middle school, driving lessons, his first shave, the senior prom, college, and a whole lot of Monday nights with two of the best friends a guy could ever have.

When Coach Shanahan wasn't looking, Nick reached

up and wiped a tear from Elway's eye. For all Nick knew, his parents had called the FBI and reported him as a missing person! At this very moment, there could be a manhunt going on! And would anybody look on the Denver Broncos' bench? No way!

And what about the real John Elway? Where was he while all this was going on? Did he know that some eleven-year-old had hijacked his body? That some stranger was reading his playbook *and* his birthday card from his parents? Elway needed his life back too. It was only fair.

Maybe he should do something. Nick thought desperately. Maybe he should go to the Denver police and explain what had happened. No, that wasn't any good. Who'd believe a crazy story like that? He'd wind up in the nuthouse.

Suddenly, Coach Shanahan's foghorn voice bellowed, *"Look out for the block! Look out for the block!"*

Nick snapped to attention. The Cowboy rushers had broken through the Denver line on the punt.

One white shirt leaped high in the air just as the ball came off the kicker's foot.

Thump! The punt was blocked. It took a crazy bounce backward and blooped into the end zone. Both teams went tearing in after it. The ball disappeared under a huge pileup of bodies.

Ninety football players and seventy-six thousand fans were on their feet. Nick held his breath and crossed his fingers and toes. The referees began pulling bodies off the pile. And when they reached the bottom—

The referee's arms shot up. "Touchdown, Dallas!"

A mammoth groan went through the stadium. Denver now trailed 21–17. Exactly fifty-three seconds remained on the clock.

"Okay, offense, get ready!" barked Shanahan.

Nick felt the coach's hand on his shoulder pad. "It's a tough spot to be in, John. But you're the master."

"You can count on me, Coach," said Nick Lighter.

One Final Desperation Drive

Nick's heart was beating so hard that he could hear the pounding echoing in John Elway's helmet. This was what it was all about—*Monday Night Football*, less than a minute to play, one final desperation drive. How many times had he sat with Coleman and Elliot in front of the TV and sweated out a moment exactly like this one? To be on the field playing it through was a thrill beyond his imagination.

He couldn't believe his teammates were so calm. In the huddle, they acted like Denver was a hundred points ahead and didn't have a worry in the world.

They've seen Elway pull off a million comebacks, he reminded himself. *The thing they don't know is—I'm not John Elway!*

Nick completed two short passes to Shannon Sharpe. Then Terrell Davis plowed straight through the defense for a thirty-yard gain, and Denver called the last of its time-outs. There were twenty-four seconds left on the clock.

"Hut-*hut!*"

The snap came early, and Nick juggled it, wasting precious seconds. By the time he dropped back to throw, the careful timing patterns were messed up. The receivers weren't where they were supposed to be!

Busted play! Nick thought. *I'll have to run it myself!*

Elway's superspeed propelled Nick around the defensive end. Dallas players were flying in all directions. Nick was just about to jump out of bounds when he thought he saw it—a clear path to the goal line thirty-five yards away. He could do it! He *knew* he could! He would be the hero and win the game for Denver!

He never saw the linebacker who blindsided him. He was hit just below the knees. As he fell, he tried to hurl himself out of bounds to stop the clock. But he couldn't make it.

Oh, no! He was down—in bounds—and time was running out! He had taken over John Elway's body only to lead the Broncos to a heartbreaking defeat!

"Line up!" howled Coach Shanahan from the bench.

Broncos scrambled from all over the field to get into formation for a quick snap. Nick threw the ball into the ground to stop the clock. There were only two seconds remaining in the game.

He was devastated. "I'm so sorry!" he blubbered in the huddle. "It's all my fault! Now we're down to our last play! I could kill myself!"

His teammates looked at him as though he had a cabbage for a head.

"That's ancient history, John," Sharpe told him.

Coach Shanahan's voice came out of the small speaker in Nick's helmet. "Fifty-three bob, odd six, on one."

He goggled. It was the same call he had heard in his "daydream" at Overlook Outdoor Center. Only this time he knew exactly how the play was supposed to work. It was a gutsy move. But could it get the Broncos thirty-one yards to the goal line for an amazing come-from-behind win?

The tension in Mile High Stadium was so thick you could almost reach out and squeeze it. The crowd noise was an uninterrupted roar. He prayed that his receivers could hear his "Hut!" in the deafening din.

The ball was snapped, and the Denver receivers charged toward the end zone. Nick had barely touched the ball when Dallas's Tony Tolbert broke through the line. There was no time to drop back, or even to think. His only hope was to . . .

Run! It wasn't a rollout; you couldn't call it a scramble. It was escape. Nick sprinted across the backfield, with Tolbert hot on his heels. He looked desperately for a receiver. But Dallas was using the "dime" defense, and blue shirts were everywhere.

He spotted Terrell Davis in the far corner of the end zone. Had Davis gone crazy? To get the ball to him, Nick would have to throw *left*—back across the entire field and thirty yards deep—all while running full speed to the right.

Nobody could throw a pass like that! It couldn't be done! It was totally impossible! Why, the only person with half a prayer of pulling it off would be—*John Elway!*

Wait a minute! The thought shot through his head like a lightning bolt. *That's me!*

With a howl of *"Broncos!"* Nick wheeled around and unloaded the ball. It screamed in over helmets and reaching hands. Davis launched himself straight up and snatched the speeding bullet out of the air.

"Touchdown!" bellowed the referee.

Wham!!

Tolbert rammed into Nick like an express train. The hit was so hard that Nick felt himself actually sailing backward. He landed off balance, with all his weight on his left foot. The ankle buckled under him.

Pain—sudden and blinding. *"Owwwww!"*

But no one could hear him as seventy-six thousand fans celebrated a miraculous victory.

In the Galloway attic, Coleman and Elliot went berserk, jumping up and down and pounding each other on the back.

"Touchdown!" they screamed joyously.

Nick's sleeping form shook suddenly awake. "What touchdown?" He leaped to his feet.

Wham!

His head banged against the sloping ceiling. As he reeled from the blow, the tiny glowing football appeared inches from his face, tracing out the number 7 in the air.

"The firefly!" shrieked Jeffrey, diving into the carton for his empty jar.

"Ow!" cried Nick, collapsing to the floor.

Floor?! What happened to the field? His eyes took in the dimly lit attic. He was back! He was Nick again!

Coleman knelt over him. "Are you okay? Should I get some ice for your head?"

"My head?" groaned Nick, grabbing at his left leg. "There's nothing wrong with my head! It's my ankle!"

"Your *ankle?*" repeated Coleman in disbelief. "But you hit your head!"

"When?"

"Just now!"

"Hey!" Elliot was still focused on the TV. "Elway's hurt! I think he injured his leg on the touchdown!"

"Where's the firefly?" wailed Jeffrey. "Aw, he's gone again!"

There was the sound of pounding feet on the stairs. Mrs. Galloway appeared, eyes blazing. "What on earth is going on here? Have you all lost your minds? It's after midnight! What's all that banging and yelling?"

"Nick hit his head!" Coleman cried urgently.

"It's my ankle," Nick insisted.

"He may be delirious," Elliot supplied. "He really conked his nut."

"I'm not delirious!" Nick winced in pain. "It really hurts!" He pulled up his pant leg to reveal his left ankle, purple and swelling.

Mrs. Galloway goggled. "Martin, phone the Lighters!" she called down the stairs. "Tell them to meet us at the emergency room! Nick's broken his ankle!"

"Really?" breathed Jeffrey. "Cool!"

"But he only bumped his head!" Coleman protested.

Mr. Galloway burst up the stairs and took a look at

the ankle. "How could this happen to a kid in a padded sleeping bag?"

Nick stared back blankly. There was no way to explain that he had hurt himself throwing the winning touchdown on *Monday Night Football*.

The first thing John Elway knew, he was riding on the injury golf cart with the Denver Broncos' team doctor.

"Take it easy, John," the doctor soothed. "We'll get some ice on that ankle."

"Ankle?" the superstar echoed. "There's nothing wrong with my ankle!"

"It's a bad sprain," the doctor continued. "I'm going to take a few X rays to rule out a fracture."

"It's fine! Look!" Elway hopped off the cart and jogged in place on the grass of the sidelines.

The doctor was astonished. "I could have sworn I saw it twist."

"It's my *head* you should worry about," number 7 told him. "See?" He pulled off his helmet.

The doctor stared. An egg-size lump showed through Elway's blond hair. "How'd you get that?"

"I hit my head," Elway replied.

"On what?"

"The ceiling!"

The doctor looked up. The only "ceiling" had stars.

"What, you bonked your conk on the bottom of the Goodyear blimp?"

"Well, I—" Elway looked puzzled. "I don't have time to think about it now. Give me an aspirin. The game's about to start."

The doctor looked at him oddly. "You really *did* hit your head, didn't you? The game's over, John."

"It *is*?"

"You threw two touchdowns and ran for a third!"

Elway thought back. He must have hit his head harder than he thought. He couldn't remember anything about football. All he had were strange impressions of a hard floor, a TV set, some kids, and a really itchy sweater. Or maybe he'd been itchy because of all those bugs. . . .

Bugs?

He looked down at the helmet in his hand. A fat orange caterpillar was marching across it, all legs churning.

He shook it off onto the grass. "Did we win?" he asked the doctor.

The man smiled. "Yes, 24–21, thanks to your usual last-minute heroics. John, you're one in a million!"

The Wigwam Slide-Launcher Crutch Ball

Nick's ankle wasn't broken. It was only badly sprained. Even so, he was the center of attention when he arrived at school on crutches on Tuesday morning.

Mr. Sargent had to laugh. "You'll do almost anything to get out of gym class, won't you?"

"What happened, Nick?" Matthew Leopold taunted. "Did you get injured during *Monday Night Football*?"

Nick smiled. This jerk would never know how right he really was.

"Hey, Nick!" Coleman and Elliot came racing up.

"Are you okay?" Coleman asked anxiously.

"Oh, sure. It's just a sprain. I should be back to normal in a few days. Listen guys, I've got something to tell you—"

"Oh no, you don't," Sarge cut him off. "I've got to let you off the hook, Nick, because you've got a note from the doctor. But these two birds are going to climb ropes today."

"Aw!" chorused Coleman and Elliot.

In a way, Nick was relieved. He needed more time to collect his thoughts—not that a thousand years would be enough to work up a sensible explanation for last night. But he had to find a way to make Coleman and Elliot believe him. He had taken part in a miracle, and he was longing to share it with somebody.

It was a busy day at Middletown Elementary School. He didn't get a chance to talk to his friends until lunch. And even then, the crowded cafeteria was no place to discuss something so secret and so important.

After school, Nick thumped along behind Coleman and Elliot. He was getting pretty good on the crutches—maybe some of Elway's athletic talent had stuck to him. The three settled themselves on their usual bench in Wigwam Park.

"Okay, Nick," said Elliot. "All day you've been looking like you were about to bust. What's the big news?"

Nick hesitated. He realized there was only one way to attack this—just say it straight out.

"Guys, I was John Elway last night."

"Right," snorted Elliot. "And I was the mighty Hercules."

"I know it sounds crazy, but I'm not kidding," Nick insisted. In a shaky voice, he told the story of the contest between the Broncos and the Cowboys, and his heroics in Elway's body.

Elliot was skeptical. "You expect us to believe that?"

"I'm *counting* on you to believe it," Nick pleaded. "I can't tell anybody else. They'd put me in the insane asylum!"

"You slept through the whole game," Elliot pointed out. "You must have dreamed all this stuff. Maybe you got a piece of bad pepperoni from the pizza."

"Wait a minute," Coleman said thoughtfully. "If he was sleeping, how come he knows everything that happened in the game?"

"I told you—I was *there!* And here's more proof. Elway sprained his ankle and wound up with a bump on the head; I bumped my head and wound up with his sprained ankle! Explain that!"

There was dead silence.

Coleman looked stricken. "Could it be?"

Elliot threw up his arms. "Now I've got two maniacs instead of just one! Guys, we've seen every *Monday Night Football* game since third grade, and none of us ever whooshed into the body of one of the players on the field! What made it happen last night?"

"I'm not a hundred percent sure," Nick admitted, "but I think it might have something to do with my grandfather's football shirt."

"The world's itchiest sweater?" Coleman asked, round eyed.

"Think about it," Nick said earnestly. "Last week I fell asleep with that thing on my face, and I had a flash of the Broncos' training room. When I wore it at Overlook, I spent a few seconds in their practice huddle. And last night I went all the way. I was Elway! I ran his offense! I looked in his locker! I read his birthday card from his folks! I even asked Al Michaels to say hi to you guys! Did he do it?"

Coleman and Elliot leaped to their feet. Each backed away a step.

"That was *you*?" Elliot croaked.

"You were John Elway," Coleman barely whispered.

Elliot's mind worked in a logical fashion. He needed reasons and explanations. "If you were *him*," he began slowly, "then who was in your body, asleep in the attic with us?"

It took a moment for this to sink in.

"*John Elway!*" cried Coleman in agony. "He was in my house, and I didn't even get his autograph!"

"And you let your brother march bugs up and down

his stomach," Elliot reminded him.

Coleman faced the founder of the Monday Night Football Club. "So what you're saying," he mused slowly, "is that you have a magic shirt."

"There's no such thing as magic," scoffed Elliot.

Nick shrugged. "I know it sounds nuts. But something sure was magic last night. Or at least really, totally, *unbelievably* cool!"

"Wow!" breathed Coleman. "Do you think your grandfather knew about it?"

"He must have," Nick replied. "Otherwise, why would he hang onto a beat-up old jersey? And why would he get the McLawyers to put it in such a safe place that they almost didn't find it?"

"I'll bet he used it himself," Elliot concluded. "For all we know, he might have switched places with some of the all-time greats! Jim Brown! Johnny Unitas! Maybe even Frank Gifford from *Monday Night Football*!"

"I always thought Grandpa didn't like me," Nick reflected. "But he must have. He left me the greatest thing he owned."

Elliot's scientific mind was in gear. "If only there was some way to test it, analyze it, see what makes it work."

Nick grinned. "There is."

They looked at him expectantly.

"Next Monday night, one of you guys can try it. As near as I can tell, all you have to do is wear the shirt and fall asleep. Any volunteers?"

"First, let's get something straight," said Elliot. "If all this is a lie, and you're messing with our heads, right now is your last chance to confess. After this there are no do-overs, and you're kicked out of the Monday Night Football Club forever."

"Scout's honor," Nick vowed, saluting with two fingers.

Coleman looked cautious. "Last night—was it fun?"

Nick glowed. "If you take all the roller coasters in the world, and build them together, and then ride them blindfolded in a rocket-powered car . . ." He sighed with contentment. "You might get one tenth of the thrill of playing in a *Monday Night Football* game."

"I'm in!" chorused Coleman and Elliot instantly.

"Good," approved Nick. "Because I just thought of how we're going to decide who goes next."

"How?" asked Coleman.

"With the Wigwam Slide-Launcher Crutch Ball."

"A trick play?" said Elliot in disbelief. "You can't even walk!"

"You guys go out deep for a pass," Nick instructed. "Whoever catches it wears the shirt next Monday." He unzipped his book bag and pulled out their football.

"Hut, hut, *hike!*"

Coleman and Elliot took off. Nick struggled to his feet. He tossed the ball up, pulled back one crutch like a baseball bat, and swung.

Pow!

The football zoomed straight for the jungle gym. It hit the slide with a clang, rocketed up the smooth slope, and shot off the top toward the two receivers.

"Me!" they both called, pushing and shoving for position.

Nick watched the trick play unfold perfectly. The Wigwam Slide-Launcher Crutch Ball dropped out of the cold autumn sky. Coleman and Elliot both jumped for it.

"I've got it!" cried Elliot.

Nick thumped toward them, laughing from pure excitement. It didn't matter which of his two friends had made the catch. Coleman would get his chance. And as for Nick, he knew that as soon as his ankle healed, he'd be back in that itchy shirt right after Coleman. This adventure was only beginning for all of them.

People said that *Monday Night Football* was exciting. Man, they didn't know the half of it!

The Official Monday Night Football Club Story
of Comeback King John Elway

For the Denver Broncos, John Elway means their team is always in the game. In fifteen NFL seasons, Elway led the Broncos to thirty-seven fourth-quarter comeback victories. To accomplish these miracles, Elway uses his arm and his feet with equal brilliance. He's the only player to pass for more than 3,000 yards and rush for more than 200 yards in eight consecutive seasons. Elway has taken the Broncos to the NFL playoffs six times, including three trips to the Super Bowl.

John Elway grew up in Granada Hills, California. He played both baseball and football in high school, and as an outfielder, helped Granada Hills High win the Los Angeles city championship. Elway was drafted in the first round by the Kansas City Royals baseball team, but decided to play football at Stanford University. His rocket arm and cat-quick feet made him one of the best quarterbacks in the nation. He set several NCAA and Pacific-10 passing records.

As a senior, Elway was nominated for the Heisman Trophy (an award that goes to the best college player). During the summer, he played baseball for a New York Yankees' minor league team. But after graduating from Stanford in 1983, he joined the Denver Broncos, forgot about baseball, and began making NFL history.

In his second season as a pro, he led Denver to a 12–2 record.

The next year he set team records for attempts, completions, and passing yardage. To reach his first Super Bowl with Denver in 1986, Elway had one of his most famous afternoons. In the AFC Championship Game against Cleveland, the Broncos were behind by a touchdown with less than six minutes to play. It was time for "The Drive." Led by Elway, the Broncos moved ninety-eight yards in fifteen plays. Elway hit Mark Jackson with a five-yard touchdown pass with just thirty-seven seconds left to tie the game. In overtime, Elway led them to the winning field goal. The next stop was Super Bowl XXI.

In 1987, Elway was the NFL's most valuable player, leading the Broncos to their second consecutive Super Bowl. In 1989, Elway and the Broncos made it to their third Super Bowl in four years. After playing for fourteen years—and in more career games than any Denver player—Elway still is going strong. In 1996, he tied his personal best with twenty-six touchdown passes and had the second-best passer rating of his career. Entering 1997, Elway ranks third all-time in career attempts, completions, and yardage.

ELWAY HONORS

Five Pro Bowls; 1993 AFC player of the year; 1987 NFL most valuable player; 1992 NFL Man of the Year; 1993 and 1996 AFC leader in passer rating.

ELWAY BY THE NUMBERS

	Att.	Cmp.	Pct.	Yards	TD	Int.	Rating
1996	466	287	61.6	3,328	26	14	89.2
Career	6,392	3,633	56.8	45,034	251	205	78.5

NFL/MONDAY NIGHT FOOTBALL CLUB FANTASY SWEEPSTAKES OFFICIAL RULES

NO PURCHASE NECESSARY

1. HOW TO ENTER: Handprint full name and address (city, state or province and zip or mail code), daytime phon
number with area code and birthdate on a 3" x 5" card; on a separate sheet of paper write an original story about
football fantasy no longer than 200 words; staple the card to the upper right corner of the first page of the story an
mail it, postage prepaid, to NFL/Monday Night Football Club Fantasy Sweepstakes, 114 Fifth Avenue, New York, N
10011, postmarked by February 2, and received by February 6, 1998.

2. ENTRY LIMITATIONS: Limit one entry per person. Story must be an original work and hand printed or type
Entries which meet all the requirements will be eligible for the sweepstakes drawing. Open only to children betwee
7 and 14 upon entering who are legal residents of the U.S.A. (excluding its territories, possessions, overseas mil
tary installations and commonwealths) or Canada (excluding Quebec) and not employees of Disney Publishing, (th
"Sponsor"), The National Football League, their parent, subsidiary or affiliated companies, the advertising, prom
tional or fulfillment agencies of any of them, nor members of their immediate families. Sponsor is not responsible f
printing errors or inaccurate, incomplete, stolen, lost, illegible, mutilated, postage-due, misdirected, delayed or la
entries or mail, or equipment or telephone malfunction.

3. RESERVATIONS: Void where prohibited or restricted by law and subject to all federal, state, provincial and loc
laws and regulations. All entries become the Sponsor`s property and will not be returned. By entering this swee
stakes, each entrant agrees to be bound by these rules and the decisions of the judges. Acceptance of prize co
stitutes the grant of an unconditional right to use winner's name, picture, voice and/or likeness for any and all pu
licity, advertising and promotional purposes without additional compensation, except where prohibited by la
Sponsor is not responsible for claims, injuries, losses or damages of any kind resulting from the acceptance, u
misuse, possession, loss or misdirection of the prize.

4.WINNER: Will be notified by mail after February 14, l997. Prize will be awarded in the name of the parent/le
guardian of the winner. Winner is required to prove eligibility. The failure of a potential winner's parent/legal guard
to verify address and execute and return an Affidavit of Eligibility/Release within ten (10) days from the date of n
fication, or the return of a notification as undeliverable, will result in disqualification and the selection of an altern
winner. All travelers will be required to execute a Release of Liability prior to ticketing. A Canadian resident wh
a winner will be required to correctly answer a mathematical skills test to be eligible to collect the prize. For the na
of winner (after February 14, l998) and/or sweepstakes rules, send a self-addressed, stamped envelope
NFL/Monday Night Football Club Fantasy Sweepstakes, 114 Fifth Avenue, New York, NY 10011. WA and VT r
dents may omit the return postage.

5.PROCEDURES: Sweepstakes begins on September 15, 1997, and ends on February 2, 1998. Winner will
selected from all eligible entries received in a random drawing on or about February 14, 1998, under the supe
sion of the Marketing Division of Hyperion Books for Children as judges. Odds of winning depend on the numbe
eligible entries received.

6.PRIZE: One (1) GRAND PRIZE: A four (4) days/three(3) nights trip for four (4) to the 1998 NFL Quarterba
Challenge (the "Event"). The date and location of the Event is yet to be determined by The National Football Leagu
The trip includes VIP seating in players' hospitality area for one (1) day at the Event, coach air transportation to/fr
the major metropolitan airport nearest to winner's home and the major airport nearest the Event, airport transfe
and hotel accommodations (one room) for three (3) nights in the city of the Event. All taxes and expenses not me
tioned herein are not included and are the responsibility of the winner. Winner must be willing to make the trip du
ing the Event, or an alternate winner will be selected. (Approximate retail value of trip: $2,000.) Prize is no
redeemable for cash or transferable and no substitution allowed except at the sole discretion of the Sponsor, wh
may substitute a prize of equal or greater value if the Event is cancelled for any reason. The prize will be awarded
NFL Films, Inc., NFL Properties, Inc., NFL Enterprises, L.P., the NFL, its member professional football team
("Member Clubs") and each of their respective affiliates, officers, directors, agents, and employees (collectively, "th
NFL") will have no liability or responsibility for any claim arising in connection with participation in this sweepstake
or offer or any prize awarded. The NFL has not offered or sponsored this sweepstakes in any way.

The Elway Foundation

One of the best things about being an NFL player is that I can use my fame to help other people. In 1987, I started an organization called The Elway Foundation. We raise money to help kids all over Colorado. Every year, the foundation holds a golf tournament and a celebrity auction. All the money raised goes to kids in Colorado who need help. Because of our many generous friends, the foundation has given more than $2 million to the Kempe Children's Center and the Family and Community Education and Support (FACES) program.

The Kempe Center helps kids who have been victims of abuse. FACES works with families to help make their lives better. Both organizations help hundreds of people every year. My wife, Janet, and I realize how many kids out there need a helping hand, and we're happy we can offer one through the Elway Foundation. You can, too.

If you or your family want more information about The Elway Foundation, you can write to us at 12835 East Arapahoe Road, Tower II, Suite 700, Englewood, CO 80112.

Thank you!

John Elway